RISE OF THE
GREEN FLAME

Written by
Bernard Mensah

Art by
Natasha Nayo

BRANCHES

SCHOLASTIC INC.

KWAME'S MAGIC QUEST

Read the next adventure!

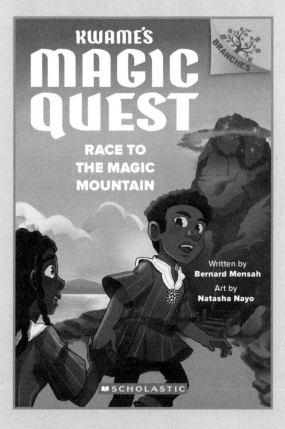

TABLE OF CONTENTS

To my two sons, Papa-Kow and Jojo, who inspire me every day
to be the best I can be. I love you and I am so proud of you!—BM

To my family who have always supported me in my artistic journey.
Thank you so much for always being my inspiration and my strength.—NN

While Kwame's Magic Quest takes place in a fantasy world, many of the places, people, clothes, names, foods, and cultures come from real African countries. The author would like to thank Adjei Kwesi Boateng for sharing his knowledge of Ghanaian culture for this book.

Text copyright © 2024 by Bernard Mensah
Illustrations copyright © 2024 by Natasha Nayo

All rights reserved. Published by Scholastic Inc., *Publishers since 1920*. SCHOLASTIC, BRANCHES, and associated logos are trademarks and/or registered trademarks of Scholastic Inc.

The publisher does not have any control over and does not assume any responsibility for author or third-party websites or their content.

Library of Congress Cataloging-in-Publication Data

Names: Mensah, Bernard (Children's author), author. | Nayo, Natasha, illustrator.
Title: Rise of the green flame / written by Bernard Mensah ; illustrated by Natasha Nayo.
Description: First edition. | New York : Scholastic Inc., 2024. | Series: Kwame's magic quest ; 1 | Audience: Ages 6–8. | Audience: Grades 1–3. | Summary: Eight-year-old Kwame is eager to start Nkonyaa School and learn calabash magic, yet none of the teachers can figure out what kind of magic is in his calabash—but when one of Kwame's new friends is possessed by an evil magic his power is revealed.
Identifiers: LCCN 2022041941 (print) | ISBN 9781338843293 (library binding) | ISBN 9781338843286 (paperback) Subjects: LCSH: Magic—Juvenile fiction. | Gourds—Juvenile fiction. | Good and evil—Juvenile fiction. | Schools—Juvenile fiction. | Friendship—Juvenile fiction. | Ghana—Juvenile fiction. | CYAC: Magic—Fiction. | Gourds—Fiction. | Good and evil—Fiction. | Schools—Fiction. | Friendship—Fiction. | Ghana—Fiction. | LCGFT: Novels.
Classification: LCC PZ7.1.M47326 Ri 2024 (print) | DDC [Fic]—dc23
LC record available at https://lccn.loc.gov/2022041941

10 9 8 7 6 5 4 3 2 1   24 25 26 27 28

Printed in the U.S.A.   206
First edition, February 2024
Edited by Katie Carella
Cover design by Brian LaRossa
Book design by Jaime Lucero

DEAR KWAME,

Welcome to the start of your magical journey!

My name is Principal Wari. I am the head of Nkonyaa (IN-kohn-YAH) School. Nkonyaa is what we call magic. Nkonyaa elders are going to be your teachers.

Every child comes here when they turn eight years old. When you arrive, you will receive a magic calabash from the Nkonyaa Tree, which you will use for spells.

calabashes

There are four types of magic calabashes. Each type has a different symbol.

 EARTH BREAKER These calabashes control soil, rocks, or anything inside the earth.

 SUN WIELDER These calabashes control fire.

 TIME BENDER These calabashes control time.

 WEATHER HANDLER These calabashes control the weather.

Students can reach four levels of magic. Magic gets harder at each level! A different symbol appears on your robe as you reach each level.

BEGINNER MAGIC	BASIC MAGIC	HALFWAY MAGIC	ADVANCED MAGIC

I look forward to meeting you soon!

Principal Wari

MEET THE CHARACTERS

Kwame

Fifi

Esi

Dela

Yaw

Papa-Kow

CHAPTER 1

READY FOR SCHOOL

Kwame woke with a wide grin on his face. Today was going to be *awesome*. He was finally going to learn calabash magic!

Everyone had magic inside them. The first day of Nkonyaa School was when eight-year-olds were given their magic calabashes and discovered their magic type.

1

Kwame danced over to the mirror and picked up his school robe. The blue fabric rippled with magic. The trim shimmered, flashing shades of gold.

Kwame struck a pose. *Woohoo! I'll finally have a real calabash!* he thought. *I can't wait to find out what kind of magic is inside me!*

He raced downstairs. "Let's go, Dad!"

"You're in a hurry!" Dad chuckled.

Mom ruffled his hair. "He's in a hurry to be a Weather Handler like his mom."

Dad clapped Kwame's back. "No, he's going to be a Time Bender like me."

"I don't know what type of magic I'll have," Kwame said, tapping his foot. "But I don't want to be the last one to the Nkonyaa Tree!"

Calabashes came from the Nkonyaa Tree, which matched the magic inside of you to a magical calabash fruit.

"Alright, alright," Dad said, gulping down his tea. "I'll prepare the spell so you can transport with me."

Dad pulled out his calabash. Its round edges were black with soot. A few streaks of copper could be seen.

He crushed purple tiger nuts into the bowl of his calabash, and the room filled with the scent of marshmallows and cinnamon. Then he sprinkled in flakes of momoni, and Kwame held his nose. The fishy mixture smelled rotten.

Dad stirred until the mixture became gloopy.

Kwame gave his mom a big hug. He wouldn't see her again until the school term ended.

"Be brave, my dear!" Mom said.

"Hold on tight, Kwame!" Dad said. He muttered the spell into his gloop-filled calabash: "Kor sukuuu hor!"

Colors flashed around Kwame. He felt like he was falling as he and his dad vanished with a *whoosh*.

CHAPTER 2

TAP TAP TAP

Kwame came to a sudden stop. His legs wobbled like jelly.

"We're here, Kwame!" Dad said.

Kwame gasped. Nkonyaa School was so tall it seemed to touch the clouds. In front of the school was a long path that forked in two. One fork led to a tiny mud hut. The other led to the magical Nkonyaa Tree. Behind the tree was a second, larger mud hut.

Leading up to the tree was a long line of other blue-robed eight-year-olds. Kwame counted forty new students, all waiting to receive their magic calabashes.

"Join the line, Kwame," Dad whispered. "Good luck!"

"Thanks, Dad. See you after the rainy season," he said, hugging him.

Dad smiled, then disappeared with a *whoosh.*

Kwame got in line behind a smaller boy with wild hair shaped like a flame. The boy was reading, not paying attention to anything going on.

Kwame was so excited he could hardly stand still. *How can he read at a time like this?* Kwame wondered.

An Nkonyaa elder wearing a rainbow-colored robe called the new students up

to the tree one at a time. The line slowly moved forward.

Kwame watched as the boy with fire-shaped hair went next.

The elder waved him over and whispered something Kwame couldn't hear. Then a calabash fruit dropped from the tree! The boy stood aside as the elder walked the calabash fruit into the tiny mud hut.

Why are the elders taking the calabashes into that hut? Kwame wondered.

Finally, an elder in a white robe waved him over. She wore a chain of wooden beads around her neck. The beads moved like they were alive. They changed color with each breath.

Wow! Kwame thought.

"My name is Ms. Dofi," she said, smiling. "Are you ready?"

Kwame nodded.

The Nkonyaa Tree towered above Kwame as Ms. Dofi led him up to its trunk. The tree's roots were twisted in a tight knot. The trunk was as wide as a bus. Mosslike fingers hung from the branches. Each leaf was striped like a candy cane. The leaves whispered in the breeze. Kwame thought they sounded like hushed voices.

"Tap here with your head three times and say 'ma me biribi' each time," she explained. "The tree will search your soul and it will drop a calabash fruit to match it."

Kwame's heart raced as he did as he was told. When his head touched the tree, his entire body buzzed.

Then the Nkonyaa Tree pulsed with a bright red light.

That can't be a good sign, Kwame thought. He took a step back.

Ms. Dofi took a step back, too. "The tree has never done that before!" she said.

CHAPTER 3
CALABASH TROUBLE

A calabash fruit dropped into Ms. Dofi's waiting hands. Then the Nkonyaa Tree stopped pulsing. Kwame tried to get a good look at his calabash, but Ms. Dofi ran it into the tiny hut without saying a word.

Kwame could hear music coming from the hut. "What happens in there?" he asked another elder.

"We play drums and dance to hollow out each magic calabash," the elder explained. "Once it's carved, the calabash will show us your magic type." She also hurried away.

Kwame joined the big crowd of students waiting to learn their magic types. The boy with fire-shaped hair was there, still reading.

Soon, calabash after calabash came out.

An elder walked over to the boy. The boy's calabash looked like white clay.

"Your magic type is Earth Breaker," the elder said to the boy, smiling.

The boy held his calabash for a minute before the elder took it back.

Kwame's wait felt like forever.

Finally, another elder waved him over. She knelt, forcing a smile. "Your calabash is not like one we've seen before. We think the flashing Nkonyaa Tree might have something to do with it. We'll need to run more checks on it to uncover your magic type."

Kwame's heart sank. *What's wrong with my calabash?* he thought.

CHAPTER 4

GREEN AND GOLD

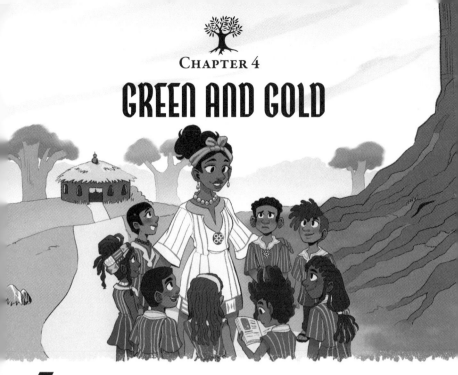

The elder walked Kwame back to the group of new students. "I'm Ms. Kumi, one of your teachers. Follow me," she said.

Ms. Kumi led the group into the larger mud hut, behind the Nkonyaa Tree.

"First, you need to learn how calabash magic started," Ms. Kumi said. "This hut, which we also call a shrine, is where it all began!"

Everyone looked around and gasped. A gleaming gold calabash sat on a pedestal. Its shine lit the whole room.

Ms. Kumi smiled. "This special calabash belonged to Okomfo Anochi. He was the very first and most powerful Nkonyaa elder. He discovered the rules of calabash magic. And his calabash—this calabash with the five symbols—is the only Omni calabash in the world."

"What's an Omni calabash?" a girl asked.

"Usually a calabash can only do one type of magic. But the Omni can create magic from all four types: Earth Breaker, Sun Wielder, Time Bender, and Weather Handler," the elder replied. "And because it is so special, it has its own symbol, too."

OMNI CALABASH

"What kind of calabash is that one?" asked the boy with fire-shaped hair, pointing to the darkest part of the shrine.

There, a calabash glowed green. It seemed to suck the brightness out of the room, like night trying to take over day.

"That is the Boni calabash," Ms. Kumi replied. "It is as old and as powerful as the Omni calabash. However, it is evil and anyone who touches it is soon swallowed by its power."

Kwame felt a chill. Everyone was quiet, their eyes fixed on the Boni calabash.

"Don't worry, students. Ancient magic stops people from touching these powerful calabashes." The elder's voice lightened. "Now it's time to eat, before we head into school. Follow me!"

Ms. Kumi led them to a grassy area and spoke a spell into her calabash.

A picnic appeared! There was lots of food, but Kwame was too worried to eat much. He just sat quietly, listening to everyone talking.

Kwame
overheard two
students
giggling
about being
Sun Wielders.
Two other
students talked
about their Earth Breaker
magic type.

After the picnic, Ms. Kumi led them all up the path to the school.

Kwame walked behind everyone else, biting his bottom lip. He was worried about what could be wrong with his calabash. *Why can't they figure out my magic type?!*

The school building towered above him. Its walls were silvery white and reflected the light from the sun. Wooden sticks stuck out from each wall and moved in all directions.

The school's dark black doors were giant. The group paused before them, waiting. Kwame stood on his tiptoes to see why everyone had stopped, when suddenly—

"Akwaaba, Kwame," said a booming voice. The school had greeted him by name!

Kwame jumped. He had never seen talking doors before.

Ms. Kumi turned to look at Kwame. "How strange. The doors normally call students to enter in the order of the group. I've never seen them call someone at the back first. But go right inside, Kwame."

Kwame took a deep breath, then walked through. *Nkonyaa School, here I come!*

CHAPTER 5
NEW BEGINNINGS

Kwame stood in a long hallway. Classrooms with large glass windows lined each side. Busy students rushed from class to class.

There must be hundreds of students here, thought Kwame.

Ms. Kumi led their group down the hall. "At Nkonyaa School, the symbol on your robe changes as you learn more magic. The star symbol means you are new to magic."

Some older students walked past. The elder pointed at them. "Those students are studying basic calabash magic. When you reach that level, the swirly symbol will appear on your robes."

Next, Ms. Kumi stopped in front of a classroom of older students drumming and singing. "They are all studying halfway magic."

As they stood there, a girl with a gold lion necklace pointed at the boy next to Kwame. "Hey, that small kid can't be old enough to be here!"

The girl beside her laughed.

As Ms. Kumi closed the door to that classroom,

Kwame glanced at the boy with fire-shaped hair. He had his head down.

Kwame whispered, "Don't listen to them."

The boy looked up and smiled.

24

Whoosh! A teenage girl suddenly appeared next to Ms. Kumi. She had a tree symbol on her robe and a big afro. "Hi, everyone! My name is Baaba."

Ms. Kumi beamed at her. "Baaba is a student here, just like you. But she is studying advanced magic, which is the last step before becoming an elder like me. I'll leave you in Baaba's excellent hands. See you all tomorrow."

"Right." Baaba smiled. "Let's get you to your dorm rooms."

A heavy, hidden door scraped open. Lights flickered in a dark stone hallway.

Kwame gulped as he followed Baaba down the hall.

CHAPTER 6

ROOMMATES

The long stone hallway opened into a wide space with super-high ceilings and tall doors lining the walls. One wall had a single-hand clock with labels on it: RAINY, WINDY, SUNNY, and SURPRISE.

Surprise? Kwame thought. Above him, fluffy clouds floated in the air.

Baaba paused to call out names as the group walked past different doors. "Yaw and Papa-Kow, this is your room." Yaw was short, with chubby cheeks. Papa-Kow was tall with locs that reached his waist.

She paused at another door. "Esi and Dela, this one is yours." Esi was dark with long braids curled up in her scarf. And Dela had short hair and wore a bead necklace.

Ping! The clock's hand moved to RAINY. A rainstorm began inside the hall!

Baaba shouted above all the squealing students. "Not to worry, I have just the thing!" Kwame watched as she dropped a dried worm into her calabash. "Apotro bra!"

Suddenly, multicolored frogs appeared in the hall. They were holding umbrellas!

The frogs hopped up onto the students' shoulders to keep them dry.

Kwame giggled as a frog hopped onto his shoulder. "Cool!"

The group continued down the hall. "Kwame, Fifi. This is your room," said Baaba.

Kwame and the boy with fire-shaped hair stepped out of the group. *So his name is Fifi!* Kwame thought. Then they smiled at each other.

Baaba turned to them. "Your families already sent your suitcases. Unpack and get ready for lights out."

As Kwame and Fifi stepped inside, their frogs disappeared. There were two beds, on opposite sides of the room.

Kwame plopped down on one bed, but he jumped up when he heard a sizzling sound. Fifi heard the same strange, sizzling noise on his side of the room.

The boys' eyes widened when they saw that their names had been magically carved in gold on their beds.

"Wow. Magic frogs, and now magic beds! I cannot wait to see what happens next!" Kwame said.

Fifi smiled shyly. "Me too."

When they finished unpacking, the lights went out. Stars glowed on the ceiling.

Kwame slipped into bed. But as he lay there, he saw a shadow move across the room.

CHAPTER 7

NEW FRIENDS

Kwame watched the shadow move toward him. Then—*tap!* A small bright light filled the room.

It was Fifi! He cupped the light in his hand. "This is a sunspot from Ajakrom." Fifi held out his hand. "Want to see?"

Kwame took the sunspot from Fifi. It felt warm. "It's amazing," he said. "Are you from Ajakrom?"

Fifi sighed. "Sort of. My dad's work takes him all over. Where he goes, I go."

"Gosh! How many places have you lived?" Kwame asked.

"Too many . . ." Fifi's face darkened. "But now I can finally stay in one place—here at Nkonyaa School."

Kwame couldn't imagine moving all the time. *How lonely.*

"It must've been hard to make friends," Kwame said. Then he pulled out his *Famous Calabash Users* magazine. "Want to see something cool? Check this out."

They huddled together to read.

"That's my grandpa," Kwame said, pointing to a picture.

"No way! Your grandpa is Ato the Sun Master?!" Fifi said, eyes wide. "Ato was the first Sun Wielder to combine the power of the sun with calabash magic!"

32

Kwame nodded, then frowned. "I thought magic would come easily to me because Grandpa is so famous. But the elders can't even tell me my magic type."

"Try not to worry. I'm sure you'll find it out tomorrow." Fifi yawned. "Bedtime I guess." He carried the sunspot to his bed.

Soon, Kwame heard a *tap!* The room went dark.

"Good night, Kwame," Fifi whispered.

"Good night, Fifi," Kwame replied.

Kwame tossed and turned, but he could not fall asleep. He was worried about his calabash. And he wondered what his first full day of magic school would be like!

CHAPTER 8
SILVER BOWLS

Kwame was confused when he woke up. *Where am I?* he thought. But then a smile stretched across his face. *Nkonyaa School!*

His mood quickly sank though—when he heard sniffling from Fifi's bed.

"Are you okay?" Kwame asked.

Fifi wiped his face. "Yeah. I just miss my dad."

Kwame sat next to him. "I miss my parents, too. But I've already made a new friend, so that's great." He grinned at Fifi, who smiled back.

"Hey, do you play Oware?" Fifi asked.

Kwame pointed at his chest. "I am an Oware champion!"

"So am I!" Fifi brought out his gameboard and said, "Bo." The Oware balls floated in the air and dropped into the board holes. "Let's play!"

The boys played until a bell rang. *Clang!*

Baaba poked her head into their room. "Time for breakfast!"

Kwame and Fifi dressed quickly and raced out to join four other students in the hallway: Esi, Dela, Papa-Kow, and Yaw.

Baaba pointed. "This way, everyone."

As new students entered the dining room, they gasped. The room held hundreds of students talking loudly and eating. Ladles with wings zipped above the tables. They swooped down to drop food into bowls.

Baaba led their group to a table and handed them empty silver bowls.

"How do we get our food?" Kwame asked. His tummy rumbled.

Baaba smiled. "Tell the bowl what you want, loud and clear."

"Really?" Dela asked.

Baaba nodded.

"Can I have koko and koose please?" Kwame asked.

Kwame watched a ladle swoop down to fill his bowl with steaming porridge. Then a plate of warm bean cakes appeared.

"My turn!" Fifi said. "Can I have the same please?"

A ladle filled Fifi's bowl next.

"This tastes so good!" Fifi said, taking a bite. "It's better than my dad's!"

"Better than my mom's!" Kwame agreed, his mouth full.

Baaba laughed. "Magic ladles are great cooks!"

When they finished eating, Baaba called for them to line up. "Let's get you all to your first class!"

CHAPTER 9
THE FIRST CLASS

Baaba led Kwame and the other new students to a set of classrooms. She split the group into two and waved twenty students into each room. "Have a great day," she said.

Ms. Kumi stood at the front of Kwame's classroom. Colorful calabashes lined the walls. Others floated in the air, bubbling and puffing out rainbow-colored smoke. Some even sparkled and glowed. There were rows of desks, and each desk held a calabash and a matching backpack.

Kwame's heart sank when he spotted the desk with his name on it. His calabash was a muddy brown color and his backpack was droopy and dull. His calabash didn't shimmer or glow.

Mine doesn't look very magical, he thought.

Fifi tapped Kwame's shoulder, smiling. "Our desks are next to each other!"

Kwame didn't say anything. He just sank into his chair.

Ms. Kumi began to speak. "Welcome to your first magic class, students! The tree gifted you each a calabash. Remember, calabashes are living things. Friends, not tools. You must offer a gift to your calabash since you are meeting each other for the first time. When it accepts your gift, you will be ready to do magic."

She gave everyone two kola nuts. "Drop the nuts into your calabash and say, 'Ye me adamfo!'"

Yaw, a Time Bender, went first. "Ye me adamfo!" he shouted. His calabash glowed white.

"Well done, Yaw!" Ms. Kumi said.

Esi, a Sun Wielder, went next. "Ye me adamfo!"

Her calabash shone bright yellow.

"Wonderful!" Ms. Kumi clapped. "Next!"

It was Fifi's turn. He didn't sound too sure. "Y-y . . . e-e-e me a . . . damfo?"

There was a sound of stones crashing against each other.

"Marvelous, Fifi!" said Ms. Kumi. "Next!"

Calabash after calabash responded to the students' gifts. It was Kwame's turn at last.

Kwame gulped. "Ye me adamfo!" he said. Nothing happened.

"Sometimes, it takes more than one try," Ms. Kumi encouraged. "Try again."

"Ye me adamfo! Ye me adamfo!" Kwame repeated.

Nothing.

"Keep trying," Ms. Kumi said.

Clang! Just then, the lunch bell rang.

CHAPTER 10

KICKED OUT?!

Kwame headed to the dining hall with Fifi, Esi, Dela, Papa-Kow, and Yaw.

"I'm sure your calabash will accept your gift after lunch," Fifi told him as they walked.

"Thanks, Fifi. I hope so," Kwame said.

The six new friends sat together. And around them, students hurried around the dining room. Kwame ducked as a ladle flew by his head.

Dela grinned kindly at Kwame. "Don't worry, magic ladles don't hurt people."

As they waited for their food, they heard a familiar voice behind them. "Look, there's Shrimpie and his friends!"

Kwame turned. It was the same older student who had teased Fifi yesterday. Students nearby laughed.

"Let it go," Kwame told Fifi.

"I wish I knew enough magic to get back at that mean girl somehow." Fifi frowned.

"But we don't, Fifi. Just ignore her," Esi agreed.

"Fine, for now," said Fifi. "But once I learn magic, they won't be laughing at me!"

Kwame and his friends ate quickly, then rushed back to class.

Ms. Kumi clapped twice to get everyone's attention. "For those whose calabashes have accepted their gifts, let's move on."

Kwame looked around. He was the only one whose calabash had yet to accept his gift.

"It is time for you all to get to know one of your calabash's special powers," Ms. Kumi explained.

Kwame wished he could move on to the next lesson. But he dropped the kola nuts into his calabash, and shouted, "YE ME ADAMFO!"

Everyone turned to look. But still, nothing happened.

Ms. Kumi walked around the classroom, guiding students. "Try growing a root by fast-forwarding time," she told Yaw.

She turned to Fifi. "Ask your calabash for a tiny mound of clay."

When she reached Kwame, she patted his back. "Keep trying."

Kwame felt his palms getting sweaty. The students around him were already doing magic.

"Ye me adamfo!" he said, over and over.

Nothing happened.

After more tries, Ms. Kumi knelt beside him. "Kwame, you should go see Principal Wari."

Kwame's heart sank. *Am I getting kicked out of school?*

Just then, Baaba entered the classroom with a *whoosh*! She helped him pack his bag and took his calabash.

As Baaba walked him out, Kwame could feel everyone's eyes on them. Fifi gave him a thumbs-up as he walked past. But Kwame wanted to sink into the ground.

CHAPTER 11

GOLD APONCHE

Principal Wari's office smelled like an old library. It looked like one, too. Shelves stretched to the ceiling, packed with ancient books. Some of the books hummed tunes. Glass bottles filled with potions burped clouds of different-colored smoke.

Baaba turned to Kwame. "Don't worry. Principal Wari will know your magic type and why you're having trouble with your calabash."

Kwame wasn't so sure.

Baaba handed Kwame's calabash to the principal, then *whooshed* away.

Principal Wari wasn't very tall. His afro was wild and gray. And on top of his head, rested a small brown monkey.

"Kwame, I've been expecting you," he said. "Come. Take a look at this." The principal brought down a bottle that held a plant.

He let sunlight fall on the sparkly plant. A gold leaf grew instantly.

"This is gold Aponche. It supercharges calabashes," the principal explained. He studied Kwame's calabash. "The Aponche should show your magic type."

Kwame stiffened. "I hope it works."

"We will see," replied the principal.

Principal Wari placed the plant inside the bowl of Kwame's calabash. Then he picked up a drum and played a beat.

Thom, thom,
boom, boom.

"Che-re-me, che-re-me," he sang.

Kwame held his breath.

Soon, the principal stopped, confused. "Hmm. That's strange. I can sense different magic types . . . But if you were a Sun Wielder, then your calabash would have created a flame as I was drumming."

Principal Wari picked up his own Sun Wielder calabash and muttered a spell, "Sor oja mframa."

A blue flame erupted from his calabash. Principal Wari scooped it into his hand! It didn't burn him.

Then he dropped the flame into Kwame's calabash. *Pop-pop-pop!* There was a popping noise as it fizzled out.

"Hmm. Very curious," the principal said, scratching his beard. "A blue flame shouldn't have gone out if your magic type was Earth Breaker. I'll need to research—"

Suddenly, there was a loud *crash* outside the office.

CHAPTER 12
DISAPPEARED

Kwame and Principal Wari rushed into the hall. They found Fifi on the floor in front of two older students. Red flames flickered in both girls' calabashes.

"Hand over the chocolate, Shrimp," the girl with the lion necklace told Fifi, not yet noticing the principal.

"No!" said Fifi.

The other girl leaned down to grab the chocolate bar from Fifi.

Principal Wari's voice boomed. "That's quite enough, Senyo and Mawuli!"

The two older students scattered.

"You will be working in the wailing gardens after class!" the principal shouted after them.

Kwame went to help Fifi up.

But Fifi pushed his hand away, dropping the chocolate bar. "I can look after myself," he said.

Principal Wari picked up the chocolate. "Here you go, Fifi."

Fifi shook his head. He rushed off without it.

Principal Wari turned to Kwame. "You should go check on your friend. I can't help you with your calabash just yet. But I'll do some reading tonight. We'll figure out your magic type." He gave Kwame his calabash and the chocolate bar, too.

"Thank you, Principal Wari," Kwame said.

Kwame dragged his feet as he headed to the dorm. He couldn't do magic. His friend kept getting picked on. And Principal Wari had no idea why his calabash wasn't working.

CHAPTER 13

FRIENDS AND CHOCOLATE

Kwame found Fifi in their dorm room.

"I'm sorry I snapped at you earlier," Fifi said. "I just hate being bullied. Every time my dad and I moved, I had to go to a new school. I was always teased for being smaller than everyone else. I thought things would be different here."

Kwame hugged his friend. "I'm sorry those girls were mean to you—and that they stole your chocolate. Here it is."

Fifi sniffled. "I bought it for you. I know your calabash hasn't accepted your gift yet. So I wanted to cheer you up."

Kwame gave him a warm smile and halved the chocolate bar for them to share.

As they finished their snack, they played another game of Oware.

Then they went to dinner.

Kwame and Fifi found seats next to Esi and Dela in the dining hall. They had fun guessing what food was in everyone's flying ladles. But Kwame noticed Fifi was quiet.

Kwame ordered his favorite. "Banku and okro soup, please."

"Same for me please," Fifi whispered.

After dinner, Fifi went straight to his desk. He started reading a very old book.

"What is that book?" Kwame asked.

Fifi didn't respond. Instead, he pushed a different book onto Kwame's desk: *A Guide to Starting Magic.*

"Thank you, Fifi," Kwame said. He also started reading.

When it was bedtime, Fifi pulled out a sunspot to continue reading. But Kwame quickly fell asleep.

Kwame strangely found himself outside the school doors. The ground was rumbling. Bits of the school and shrine were falling down. Dark clouds filled the sky. Lightning flashed, thunder boomed, and rain poured from the sky.

People panicked, pointing at the Nkonyaa Tree and yelling, "The Omni calabash is gone!"

Kwame woke up panting. *That nightmare was so real!*

It took him a long time to fall back to sleep.

CHAPTER 14

GLOW!

When Kwame woke up the next morning, Fifi's bed was empty. So he quickly dressed and headed to the dining hall. Dela, Esi, Yaw, and Papa-Kow were there. But Fifi wasn't. No one had seen him.

When Kwame got to class, he found Fifi at his desk.

"There you are! You missed breakfast," Kwame said.

Fifi said nothing.

"Fifi?" Kwame said.

Classmates streamed in. Kwame thought Fifi looked like he might be sick.

Fifi's hand shot up. "Can I be excused?"

Ms. Kumi nodded.

Fifi grabbed his calabash and rushed out. Kwame worried something was wrong.

Just then, Ms. Kumi knelt beside Kwame. "Principal Wari hasn't found out anything new about your calabash yet. But he'll call for you when he does. Keep trying to get your gift accepted for now."

Then she turned to Kwame's classmates. "In today's lesson, you will learn to hear your calabash's voice and sense its feelings. Music helps."

She thumped a drum.

Thom,

BOOM.

Thom.

Kwame watched as Esi communicated with her calabash. It floated in the air, and a yellow flame shot from its center.

Papa-Kow communicated with his calabash, too. A small whirlwind whizzed in its center.

"Woah!" Papa-Kow said.

"Good work, students! Focus on the sound of the music," Ms. Kumi said, drumming. "Listen for your calabash."

Kwame wanted to communicate with his calabash. But it had to accept him first.

"Ye me adamfo," he said quietly, not wanting his classmates to hear.

Nothing happened.

Kwame frowned. *Everyone else is already doing magic while I'm still stuck on the first lesson!* He felt tears sting his eyes.

Frustrated, Kwame threw the kola nuts into his calabash. "Ye me adamfo!" he yelled.

At last, his calabash began to glow.

CHAPTER 15

BONI CALABASH

Kwame's calabash was glowing bright gold. It had accepted his gift of kola nuts. He was finally ready to do magic!

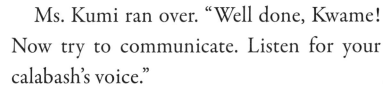

"Woohoo!" Kwame cheered.

Ms. Kumi ran over. "Well done, Kwame! Now try to communicate. Listen for your calabash's voice."

She picked up the drum.

Thom, thom, BOOM.

Kwame closed his eyes and focused on the music. The drum grew quieter, and a soft voice called his name, "Kwame."

Hello? Kwame responded in his mind.

CRASH! A loud noise snapped him back. Everyone raced out into the hallway. Fifi was lying there, his calabash spinning next to him. His clothes were singed and part of his robe still had magic flames on it.

Senyo and Mawuli, the mean older students, were there—with red flames in their calabashes.

"Grilled Shrimp!" Senyo said, laughing.

Fifi stood, facing the two girls with his fists balled up. "Leave me alone . . . or else!"

A flame roared from Senyo's calabash. "Or else what?" She laughed again.

"Let me through!" Ms. Kumi said, pushing through the crowd of students. "Stop this! That is enough!"

Fifi opened his backpack, mumbling, "I warned them."

He pulled out a calabash—but it was not his own. It was dark green.

The Boni calabash?! Kwame gasped. He could feel the evil seeping from it.

Ms. Kumi stepped back. "Drop that calabash!" she shouted at Fifi.

But Fifi turned and pointed the Boni calabash at Senyo and Mawuli. "Bo no!" he shrieked.

A green bolt leaped toward them. They tried to dodge it, but the bolt hit them.

They both dissolved into puddles!

Kwame's jaw dropped. *What did Fifi just do?!*

CHAPTER 16

GONE

Ms. Kumi stepped forward. "Fifi! Drop that calabash at once!" she shouted.

"Bo no," Fifi said the spell again. This time, he pointed at Ms. Kumi.

A green bolt dissolved her, too.

Students screamed and scattered, but Kwame couldn't move.

Principal Wari pushed through the crowd. "Get behind me, students!" he shouted as he put his calabash on the floor and spoke a spell. "Ma me ahoudin!"

A massive wall of flames shot out of the principal's calabash. Kwame could feel the heat as the flames roared toward Fifi.

69

"Hahahahaha!" Fifi cackled in a strange, deep and gravelly voice. "Fire won't stop me!" He waved his hand, and the wall of fire disappeared.

Kwame shouted, "Fifi, stop—"

But then Fifi turned to him.

Kwame gasped. Fifi looked like a green-eyed monster with green hairy skin and sharp teeth.

Fifi growled at Kwame, "Bo no."

Two green bolts headed toward Kwame!

Kwame closed his eyes and held his calabash up in front of him and—

Nothing happened. Kwame opened his eyes. He wasn't a puddle. But his calabash was shaking! Inside it, a green whirlpool swirled.

Kwame saw the principal looking at him.

Fifi shrieked in fear. Then he transformed into a towering green flame and flashed out of an open window.

Kwame raced to the window. "Fifi, wait!" But his friend was gone.

CHAPTER 17

PUDDLE PEOPLE

Kwame looked around. There were three green puddles on the hallway floor.

Those puddles used to be people, Kwame thought.

Principal Wari took two bottles from his robe. He poured them into his calabash.

Then he called to Ms. Dofi, "Get our drums and bring your calabash!"

When Ms. Dofi returned, she and Principal Wari sat with their legs crossed. They began to beat their drums.

BOOM. BOOM, boom, THOM.

BOOM, boom, THOM.

As they played, they sang, "Gi nkwa, Gi nkwa, Gi nkwa."

A purple flame leaped from Principal Wari's calabash into Ms. Dofi's calabash. Again and again. The flame grew with each hop.

Then Principal Wari stopped

drumming. He pointed at the puddles.

The purple flame danced on each puddle. As it did, the puddles bubbled and released purple smoke.

When the smoke cleared, Senyo and Mawuli stood in the hallway. They looked stunned.

Kwame heard a cough nearby and turned to see Ms. Kumi. She was holding her head.

Kwame breathed a sigh of relief—until the walls began to shake! Part of the wall beside him came crumbling down.

"Get outside, everyone!" Principal Wari shouted.

CHAPTER 18

STORMS AND MAGIC

The ground rumbled beneath Kwame's feet as he raced outside. Dark clouds filled the sky. Thunder boomed. A mighty wind blew the branches of the Nkonyaa Tree. Heavy rain began to pour.

Ms. Dofi raced from the shrine, shouting, "Both calabashes have been stolen!"

Kwame felt a chill go through him. *This feels familiar. It's like what happened in my nightmare.*

Principal Wari's eyes landed on Kwame. "It's time. We must talk about your calabash."

"Now?" Kwame asked, the rain soaking him.

Principal Wari nodded. "This way," he said.

He led Kwame into the shrine. "The world is in trouble," the principal explained.

"Those two calabashes need to be returned to the shrine. All magic will disappear without them in their proper place. And without magic, the school, the shrine, and eventually the world will all crumble!"

76

Principal Wari continued. "The Boni calabash is too powerful for *anyone* to handle—let alone a first-year student. Anyone who uses it becomes a green-eyed monster. I am not sure how Fifi got past the spells that stop people from touching those calabashes. It is practically impossible to read the ancient spell books."

Kwame snapped his fingers. "Fifi was reading an old book last night. That must've been an old spell book!"

Principal Wari paced. "Interesting. A student should not be able to read those spells . . ." He turned to Kwame. "How did you stop the green bolt earlier?"

Kwame shrugged. "I don't know. My calabash saved me."

Principal Wari paused, deep in thought. "Through my research, I learned that there is only one kind of calabash that can do what yours did today. You and your calabash may be the key to saving this world's magic."

"*I* could be the key?" Kwame asked. "But I can't even do beginner magic."

Principal Wari looked at him. "Kwame, your friend is in danger. He needs you."

Kwame used his bravest voice. "Then I will help!"

The ground rumbled again, and a piece of the wall fell near Kwame.

Principal Wari drew on the mud floor.

He placed his calabash on the mark. "We don't have much time. You must speak to Okomfo Anochi."

"The elder who discovered the rules of calabash magic?" Kwame asked.

Principal Wari didn't answer. He dropped Edjegua leaves into his calabash. "Fre no bra. Fre Okomfo bra," he said.

A cloud of gray smoke rose from the calabash. The smoke twisted and grew into the shape of a door.

Kwame took a step back.

Principal Wari stood. "This door leads to Okomfo Anochi, the first Nkonyaa elder. He will teach you about your calabash."

The ground rumbled again and the smoke door flashed.

"You must trust me," said the principal. "Go now, Kwame!"

Before he could change his mind, Kwame took a running jump through the door.

CHAPTER 19
OKOMFO ANOCHI

Kwame was standing in a forest near a riverbed. The air smelled like fresh-cut grass. There was a tall man nearby, washing a calabash in the river. He had an Akrafena sword tied to his back.

The man smiled when he saw Kwame. "Welcome, Kwame. I am Okomfo Anochi."

"How do you know who I am?" Kwame asked. "And where are we?"

Okomfo chuckled. "I know you because you have an Omni calabash. And you are visiting a memory of mine. This is one of my favorite places."

Kwame could not believe his ears. "My calabash is an *Omni*?" he asked.

Okomfo nodded. "Yes, it is. I can see your magic."

"But I thought only one Omni calabash existed! I have so many questions for you," Kwame said.

Okomfo shushed him. "Later, Kwame. We don't have much time. Believe in your magic. If you believe, you will be more powerful than I ever was."

Okomfo handed him a kola nut. "Here, take a bite."

As Kwame bit into the nut, a jolt of electricity ran through him.

"That wasn't a normal nut," Kwame said.

"I added a little something that will help you later," Okomfo replied. "Good luck, Kwame." With that, Okomfo turned to smoke and the sky flashed bright red.

Suddenly, Kwame was in the shrine with Principal Wari. The ground was still shaking.

Kwame felt different since eating the strange kola nut. His body tingled . . .

CHAPTER 20

READY!

Without thinking, Kwame sat down with his calabash and began to chant, "Jae bibia, jae bibia, jae bibia!"

Soon, the shaking stopped.

Principal Wari clapped. "Very well done, Kwame! That powerful stay-same spell will keep everything the same for a short while. Only an Omni calabash can cast that spell— so your calabash must be an Omni!"

"It is!" Kwame beamed.

Principal Wari scratched his beard. "That is good news. We will need its power to restore the natural balance of magic before it's too late."

"But I don't know magic!" Kwame said.

The principal knelt beside Kwame. "I'm going to teach you everything I know. You are the only one who can get both calabashes back from the green-eyed monster. Are you ready?"

Kwame took a deep breath. *I know my friend Fifi is not a monster. I need to save him . . . and the world.*

All of a sudden, Kwame heard his calabash in his head: *Believe in your magic.*

Yes, Kwame thought. *I know what to do.*

He turned to the principal. "I believe in my magic. I'm ready!"

DID YOU KNOW?

Kwame's Magic Quest is based on parts of African culture. Ghana, a country in West Africa, is where Kwame's story starts.

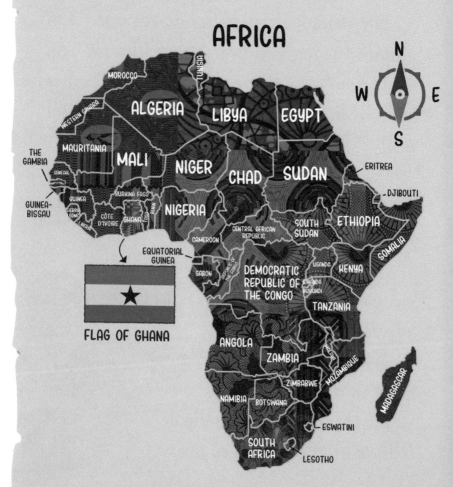

AFRICA

FLAG OF GHANA

Most people in Ghana belong to one of many ethnic groups. These groups are like your family, but bigger. Each group has their own beliefs, traditions, and languages. There are more than eighty languages spoken in Ghana alone! This book series draws inspiration from an ethnic group called the Akan.

The Akan, like most ethnic groups in Africa, believe in gods and spirits who choose special people to speak for them. In Ghana, Nkonyaa experts learn to listen to the god or spirit to tell people what the god or spirit wants.

In Kwame's Magic Quest, there is a special person named Okomfo Anochi. In real life, Okomfo Anokye was a powerful Nkonyaa user. His magic won wars in the 1600s! And he used his magic to bring a golden stool from the sky. That stool is kept in a safe place in Ghana today.

As you read this series, you will learn about Akan, Ghanaian, and African culture—and of course, magic!

LEARN MORE!

Nkonyaa (IN-kohn-YAH): Nkonyaa means magic in a language called Twi (chwee) that is spoken by most Akans. It's the perfect name for a magic school inspired by Ghanaian and African beliefs! All the spells in the book use real Twi words! Here's one and its meaning:

⭐**Apotro bra! (AH-POH-troh brah):** "Apotro" (real spelling Apɔtrɔ) means "frog." And "bra" means "come." So together, it means "come frogs."

Adinkra (Ah-DIN-krah) symbols: These special symbols have great meaning amongst the Akan in Ghana as well as across parts of Ivory Coast where there is a significant Akan population. They are typically found on clothes and decorations. Here's the name and meaning of the symbol you see on Kwame's robe:

⭐**Sesa Wo Suban:** A new start or transformation. (Fitting for beginner-magic students!)

Oware (oh-WAH-reh): Oware (Ghana), also called Ayo (Nigeria) or Awale (Ivory Coast), is a game loved across many West African countries. But in real life, the balls don't float!

Kola nuts: Kola nuts are part of most magic ceremonies in West Africa. Also traditionally, giving and receiving kola nuts are ways of welcoming people and bringing people together.

Akrafena sword: This sword is one of a group of special swords used by the Ashanti King's guards during royal ceremonies. It means bravery, strength, and power.